To the good people of "the Good Earth,"
Terrebonne Parish, Louisiana —C.S.R.

For my loving parents, Robert and Margaret Dunlavey
and stepmom Fran Lockwood Dunlavey —R.D.

Library of Congress Cataloging-in-Publication Data
Rose, Caroline Starr.
Over in the wetlands / Caroline Starr Rose ; illustrated by Rob Dunlavey.
— First edition.
pages cm.
Summary: Various wetland creatures, from alligators to egrets, enjoy what begins as a
calm and peaceful day in the bayou, then prepare for and endure a passing hurricane,
and finally settle in for a peaceful night.
ISBN 978-0-449-81016-3 (hc) — ISBN 978-0-449-81017-0 (glb) —
ISBN 978-0-449-81018-7 (ebook)
[1. Wetland animals—Fiction. 2. Animals—Fiction. 3. Water birds—Fiction.
4. Birds—Fiction. 5. Bayous—Fiction. 6. Hurricanes—Fiction.]
I. Dunlavey, Rob, illustrator. II. Title.
PZ7.R71464Ove 2015
[E]—dc23 2013018301

The text of this book is set in Weiss.

The illustrations in this book were rendered in watercolor, ink,
pencil, paint, collage, and Adobe Photoshop.

Book design by Rachael Cole

MANUFACTURED IN CHINA

1 3 5 7 9 10 8 6 4 2

First Edition

With the publication of this book, the author has made a donation to a wetland restoration organization.

Over in the Wetlands

A Hurricane-on-the-Bayou Story

written by CAROLINE STARR ROSE illustrated by ROB DUNLAVEY

schwartz & wade books · new york

Over in the wetlands
where the silky mist weaves,
Dragonfly lights on a slender reed.
Bending toward the bayou,
she dips one wing,
rippling the water as it creeps downstream.
Gentle as a whisper too soft to hear,
a faint breeze hints that a storm draws near.

Over in the wetlands
where the cypress rise,
cotton tufts dot the coastal skies.
Crab and her babies scuttle in the swells;
the wind stirs moss like silent bells.

Along the shore
the waves increase.
Pelicans scoop herring
for the littlest beaks.

Swirling the shallows,
the spoonbills stalk,
the cypress salted
with an egret flock.

Over in the wetlands
where the bayous run,
Alligator minds her restless ones.
As she rises from the waters
through the duckweed gauze,
two clamor on her head;
three ride inside her jaws.

Mama Gator feels the coming storm,
wants her babies snug and warm.
She lumbers slowly toward her den
and nestles her gatorlings deep within.

Angry clouds are gathering low.

Water churns in the undertow.

Fish dive deep; they sense the squall.

The hurricane stirs,

the hurricane crawls.

Wind-whipped waves
smash up debris.
Turtles swim for safer seas.
Dark clouds snarl, press down the skies.
The hurricane grumbles,
the hurricane writhes.

Egrets cower between cattails
from pelting sand and screaming gales.
Frothing sea-foam streaks the shore;
the hurricane twists,
the hurricane roars.

Marsh grass clutches the sandy loam;
tupelos crack, willows moan.
Floodwaters rise, rain streams down;
the hurricane drenches,
the hurricane drowns.

Pounding,

wailing,

hours endless.

Blasting,

breaking,

storm's relentless.

Over in the wetlands
where the bulrushes dance,
clouds fade over the great expanse.

At last winds ease to gentle breaths.
The hurricane yawns,
the hurricane rests.

Black Bear shambles from her home,
whuffles to her cubs they're free to roam.
Little ones tumble; their noses poke,
ambling upon a downed live oak.

Over in the wetlands
where the sun sinks red,
though branches dangle like broken threads
and the edge of sea and earth's a blur,
babies skitter to their mama,
a swamp chauffeur.

Over in the wetlands
where the stillness sighs,
turtles glide under ruby skies.
Pelicans cuddle in Mother's wings.
Mama nuzzles her gatorlings.

Over in the wetlands
in the dead of night,
Dragonfly flits through the starry light.
The swampland stretches all around,
jumbled,
peaceful,
steady,
sound.

Author's Note

This story takes place in the Mississippi River Delta, a part of Louisiana's coastal wetlands. Wetlands are low-lying areas that are completely underwater for at least part of each year. They can be found all over the world near rivers, lakes, and oceans, or on otherwise dry land where water bubbles up from underground.

One of the most biologically diverse ecosystems on earth, wetlands are home to a large number of plant and animal species. But because of habitat destruction, many of these plants and animals are in danger. Over a third of our country's threatened or endangered species make their homes in wetlands, and nearly half live in wetlands for at least part of their lives.

Wetlands function as natural speed bumps for tropical storms and hurricanes. They lessen the impact of flooding by absorbing and dispersing water, and they help control coastal erosion by weakening the force of ocean currents.

Louisiana's wetlands are made of marshes, which are home to grasses, and swamps, which are filled with woody plants and trees such as cypress, live oak, and willow. The soil of both marshes and swamps is nutrient rich. Because the slow-moving water is oxygen poor, plant matter doesn't completely decay, leaving the water a muddy coffee color.

Some of Louisiana's wetlands have been drained for building or farming. Digging navigation canals and dredging for gas and oil have destroyed even more swamps and marshes. As a result, salt water from the Gulf of Mexico has intruded on many of the state's freshwater areas, altering these ecosystems irreversibly. Since the 1930s, Louisiana has lost almost 2,000 square miles of wetlands (about 968,000 football fields), making flooding an even greater threat to Louisiana's low-lying coastal communities.

Louisiana's wetlands—home to endangered and threatened plants and animals, a place of protection and replenishment, a source of much of the United States' shrimp, crab, and oysters—face years of difficulty ahead. To learn more, visit these websites:

americaswetland.com (America's Wetland Foundation)
basinkeeper.org (Atchafalaya Basinkeeper)
lacoast.gov/new/ (Coastal Wetlands Planning, Protection and Restoration Act)
mississippiriverdelta.org (Restore the Mississippi River Delta)
epa.gov/owow/monitoring/nationswaters/waters.pdf (What's Up with Our Nation's Waters?)

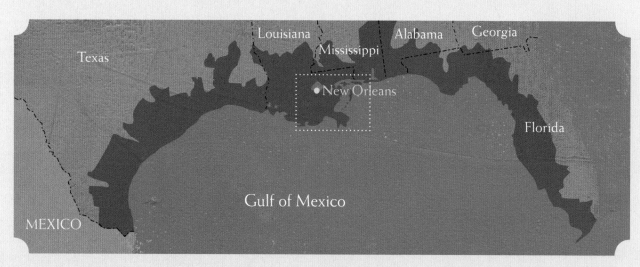

On this map, the dark green area represents the coastal wetlands of the Gulf of Mexico. This story is set in the Mississippi River Delta, which is the area featured in the rectangle.

More About the Animals in This Book

Dragonflies hatch from eggs underwater and live as naiads, or aquatic nymphs, for up to five years. When they are ready to undergo metamorphosis, they climb a leaf, twig, or reed and break out of their old skin, living only a few months more in their adult form.

Brown pelicans are Louisiana's state bird. They plunge into the ocean to fish, stunning their prey on impact and scooping it up in their basketlike beaks. Both mother and father use their webbed feet to keep their eggs warm, and they take turns feeding their hatchlings.

Snowy egrets are immediately recognizable, with their white bodies, black beaks, black legs, and yellow feet. When in flight, their necks curve like the letter S.

Like the snowy egret, the roseate spoonbill feeds in shallow waters. Spoonbills swing their submerged beaks back and forth and snap them shut when they feel prey. Unlike egrets, they fly with their necks outstretched.

Blue crab mothers carry their eggs on their undersides until they hatch. Because blue crabs have an exoskeleton, they must molt, or shed their outer shell, as many as twenty-five times before reaching maturity.

Not only do alligator babies ride on their mother's back and head, they willingly climb into her mouth! Much like chicks, baby gators begin to peep before they hatch and use a temporary egg tooth to break through their shell.

Louisiana black bear litters typically include two cubs, which stay with their mother throughout their first year. These bears make their dens in hollow trees or under fallen logs and go through a period of winter dormancy.